FIRE AND WATER

FIRE

AND

WATER

AND OTHER HAWAIIAN LEGENDS

retold by BARBARA LYONS

illustrated by BETTY RICE

CHARLES E. TUTTLE COMPANY
Rutland ‡ Vermont ‡‡ Tokyo ‡ Japan

Representatives

For Continental Europe:
BOXERBOOKS, INC., *Zurich*
For the British Isles:
PRENTICE-HALL INTERNATIONAL, INC., *London*
For Australasia:
PAUL FLESCH & CO., PTY., *Melbourne*
For Canada:
M. G. HURTIG, LTD., *Edmonton*

These stories have appeared in the *Maui News*.
Earlier versions of five of them have also appeared in
the *Honolulu Advertiser*.

Published by the Charles E. Tuttle Company, Inc.
of Rutland, Vermont and Tokyo, Japan
with editorial offices at
Suido 1-Chome, 2-6, Bunkyo-ku, Tokyo

Copyright in Japan, 1973
by Charles E. Tuttle Co., Inc.

Library of Congress Catalog Card No. 72-88932
International Standard Book No. 0-8048-1092-3

First printing, 1973

PRINTED IN JAPAN

For BARRY and ANDERS
McGREW and BONNIE

CONTENTS

1

FIRE AND
WATER

Pele, the goddess of fire, stood near her home in Puʻu Laina and regarded it critically. It was a nice little pit, yes. Warm and cozy when her fire was burning, and the view down the hillside was delightful. Yet Pele yearned for something larger, and at a more commanding height.

Slowly she turned and walked up the steep grade of the mountain on whose slopes the volcanic cone, Puʻu Laina, stood. This was Mauna Kahalawai, the Meeting Place between Heaven and Earth—a range of towering peaks, and valleys with sheer ridged walls on which grew the pale-leafed *kukui* tree and the silvery *koa*. Pele might have been quite happy here, had it not been for what she could see from the summit.

"Hale-a-ka-la," she whispered to herself. "House of the Sun." Entranced, she gazed across at the great mountain that rose in majesty beyond the plain.

Several times Pele's enemy, the sea goddess Na-maka-o-Kaha'i, had driven her from homes on other islands, islands that she had built up with her lava. But this time she would move because she wanted to, and not to another island.

How powerful she could be from such a height! When her lava had raised Hale-a-ka-la even higher, she would be able to look down on all the world; yet she could retire when she liked into the mists that so often shrouded the upper slopes—mists that would mingle with the clouds of her own smoke.

Swiftly she ran down the hillside and put out her fire, then set out on the long trip. Through a precipitous valley of Mauna Kahalawai, across the plain of Kulaka-ma'-oma'o, the Place Where the Heat Waves Shimmer. Then up the long, gradual ascent to the top of the world. She hurried through the clouds that lay on the mountainside like a damp veil.

"How I hate dampness," she muttered, trying to wipe the moisture from her arms and to shake it from her feet. "Getting my feet wet is the worst of all!"

But when she reached the mountain's top, she was glad of the clouds. She hoped that they would wrap her in secrecy as she worked, and that before Na-maka-o-Kaha'i knew what was happening, billows of volcanic smoke would hover above Pele's new home.

The sea goddess, however, had very sharp eyes. From her watery home, she saw the goddess of fire vanish into the bank of clouds.

"What can that Pele be up to?" she asked herself, watching uneasily for the other to reappear.

Pele worked hard, hidden by the dense clouds, and in time she had dug herself an enormous crater and lighted a fire in it. It became beautifully warm, and she basked in her glorious new home.

"I will call this Lua Pele," she said, "the Crater of Pele."

When Na-maka-o-Kaha'i saw the rising smoke, glowing red as it reflected Pele's fire, she was furious. She called her pet sea dragon to her and said, "Let us go and destroy our enemy. Think how she must be gloating over this, up there!"

"But she's so high," protested the dragon. "So far from the lovely wet ocean." And he flipped his tail and glided deep into the water.

It took the sea goddess several days to find him. "He's so naughty!" she complained to herself as she searched. "I don't know why I put up with him." But she did know, really, for of all her dragons, he was the fiercest when aroused.

At last, she spied him hiding under the edge of a coral reef at the bottom of the sea, and grabbed his tail as he tried to slip away.

"Oh well, I'll come if I must," grumbled the dragon. "But let go of my tail, please."

When they reached the surface, Hale-a-ka-la lay steeped in sunshine.

"It's too hot now, you see?" sputtered the sea goddess. "We'd roast under that sun. And besides, she'd see us coming—we'll just have to wait."

Finally, the conditions seemed just right. A day came

when heavy mists banked the higher slopes of the mountain, and the sun was pale behind a cloud in the sky.

They crossed the plain in a rush, leaving a wet trail behind them. When they reached the mists, they went slowly while the cool, delicious vapors replenished their supplies of moisture. They could hear the roar of a river of lava as it spilled out through a gap in the side of Pele's crater.

The sound excited the dragon, and water began to pour from his nose and mouth. The heat was terrific. Flames crackled as they leaped into the air about Pele, and tongues of fire darted out to surround her attackers.

"Ouch!" cried the sea goddess, and the dragon deluged Pele with a great stream of water.

A sound of sizzling took the place of the crackling of fire.

"Oh, oh!" wailed Pele, as the beast drenched her with a spray until her long hair clung wetly about her. "This dreadful water all over me, and on my lovely fire!" Poor Pele! She hated getting her feet wet, and here she was, soaked.

"This is sure to be the finish of you!" hissed the sea goddess.

"Never!" stormed Pele.

But she was right. With Pele soaked and miserable, it was easy for the sea goddess to conquer her. Na-maka-o-Kaha'i ordered her dragon to attack, and he tore Pele limb from limb, and flung the parts of her body far and wide. One of her leg bones flew over the edge of the mountain, where it lay at Kahiki-nui in a long mound of

lava. The *menehune,* the little men, came to see, and left their tiny footprints beside it.

Other parts of Pele's body sailed toward the end of the mountain, and formed the hill known as Na-iwi-o-Pele, the Bones of Pele.

But the goddess's spirit traveled across the channel to the island of Hawai'i, and there she made her home in a great volcano. Lua Pele, her crater on Maui, remains at the top of Hale-a-ka-la, where the memory of her ancient fire lives on in the colors of the volcanic cones.

2

LAKA AND THE MENEHUNE

A boy named Laka lived in Ki-pahulu on Maui island. He was the son of a chief, and was adored by his parents and grandmother. In fact, they rather spoiled him. He was always given what he wanted, and the older members of the family would excuse themselves by saying, "He's such a fine, handsome boy. He deserves to be happy."

So when Laka expressed a wish for a certain type of sea shell that he had seen, but which could not be found on the sands of Maui, his father set off in his canoe to cross the channel.

"There are some of those shells on the beaches of Hawai'i," he said. "Or I can find one on the ocean floor. Take care of your mother and grandmother, now."

But Laka had never thought of taking care of anyone but himself, and he spent his days watching for his father's return with the sea shell. His mother and grandmother got along very well on their own, but once in a while the old lady would look at Laka rather sadly and shake her head.

"Do you think we're bringing up the boy as we should?" she asked her daughter.

"Goodness, yes!" said Laka's mother. "See what a fine-looking lad he is!" and she went off in search of some of his favorite *'ohelo* berries.

Each morning, Laka would stand on the beach and look out across the rippling blue ocean to the mountains of Hawai'i, and wonder when his father's canoe would appear.

One day, when the air was so clear that the other island seemed only a short swim away, the thought crossed his mind that his father might be in trouble. For the first time in his life, he began to worry about another person. Surely, if all had gone well, his father would have been home long before this. And it was for Laka's sake that he had gone.

The boy continued to scan the expanse of waves for a canoe. Sometimes he sighted one, and watched excitedly until it came close enough to be recognized. But it was never his father returning home; and each time he felt more unhappy than the time before. "Something must have gone wrong," he thought.

He noticed now that his mother was looking worried. "What can I do?" he wondered. "I will ask the wisest person I know." And he went to his grandmother.

"I think the time has come for me to go in search of my father," he said to her. "I'm afraid that something has happened to him. But how can I go? My father took our only canoe."

His grandmother looked at him in silence for a moment. Then she said, "I'm glad to see, boy, that you are growing up and are beginning to think about your responsibilities. Yes, your father must be in trouble; he needs you, I feel sure. Even if he should be dead, he would need you to bring his bones back to Ki-pahulu. Do you think that you could build yourself a canoe, if I told you where to find the right tree?"

"Oh, yes, Grandmother. Feel my muscles. I'm really very strong—and I have watched the men making canoes."

"Go then up into the mountains. Look for the tree whose leaves are the shape of the moon when it is like a twisted strand of *olona*. And be sure the trunk of the one you choose is big enough around to be made into a canoe."

Laka walked up into the cool, dark forest above his home. After roaming among the trees for some time he came upon a grove of large *koa*, and picked one whose trunk was tall and straight, and thick enough for a canoe. Its crescent-shaped leaves, at the top where sunlight struck them, were silvered like tiny new moons.

"This is just the one!" said Laka to himself, and set to work with his axe.

Chopping down a big *koa* tree is slow work for a single boy, and dusk was gathering by the time it fell to the ground with a great crash. Laka straightened up and looked at it with pride, then he ran down the darkened slopes. It was scary in the forest with night coming on, and once or twice he thought he heard voices whispering. But when he looked over his shoulder, he could see nothing but the rows and rows of trees. I must have imagined it, he thought. It was only the breeze stirring the branches.

Next morning when he returned, planning to begin the task of hollowing out the log for his canoe, Laka stared about him in bewilderment. He dropped the stone adzes he had brought with him, and turned slowly around. Surely it should be right here, where he stood? But there was no fallen tree.

He must have mistaken the place, though he had been so sure. Much puzzled, he selected another *koa* and spent the day in cutting it down. This time he made a little mark on the tree next to it.

Again, on the way home, he thought he heard those whispering voices. And again, the next day, his fallen tree was not there. He knew he was in the right place because of the mark he had made.

"This can't go on," thought Laka, angry at having done two days' hard work with nothing to show for it. And each day wasted made it that much longer before he could set out to find his father. He had to think of a way to discover what was happening to the trees he cut down.

Before felling the next one he dug a huge hole next to it, and then began to chop so that it would fall into the hole. Toward evening, with a thunderous roar and a great swishing of branches, the tree settled into Laka's trench. He jumped down and hid himself among the thousands of slender leaves.

After a time he heard voices, not whispering now but chattering, as if those who were speaking did not expect

to be overheard. Who could it be, and what were they saying? They were talking about lifting Laka's tree back onto its stump! He guessed now that these were the *menehune*, the little men who worked by night and disappeared at daylight into their secret haunts. The *menehune* could be a great help when they wanted to be, finishing an enormous job in a single night. And they could do an equal amount of mischief.

Lying very still under his canopy of leaves, Laka listened as the little men chanted to their gods, asking help in what they were about to do:

> "O the four thousand gods,
>   The forty thousand gods,
>   The four hundred thousand gods,
>   The file of gods,
>   The assembly of gods!
>   O gods of these woods,
>   Of the mountain,
>   And the knoll,
>   And the water-dam,
>   O come!"

Soon more and more little men were swarming about the tree, and there was a hum of voices. They were trying to raise the tree, but it was harder to get it up out of its trench than if it had been lying on the slope.

Laka, knowing he would soon be discovered, jumped up suddenly and caught two of the *menehune*, one in each hand. "I'm going to kill you for putting my trees up again!" he cried angrily. "How dare you spoil all my work? I have to go to Hawai'i to find my father and I need a canoe."

"If you kill us," said one of the *menehune*, "no one will help you make this canoe or get it down to the beach. Even if you can make it, how are you going to drag it down the mountainside alone? It's going to be heavy, you know."

"Well. . . ." As a matter of fact, this very thing had been worrying the boy. His family had no close neighbors.

"If you will spare us," said the other little man, "and if you will build a *halau* near your house for the canoe and also arrange a feast for us, we'll make the canoe and carry it down."

"We like to see a boy who wants to help his father," said the first.

"All right. Good! I'll let you go. I don't mind telling you, I certainly could use your help."

Laka sped down through the trees. His mother was out of doors, watching for him.

"Oh, thank goodness!" she cried. "Whatever made you so late?"

Quickly, he told her about the *menehune*, and asked her to gather things for the feast. It must include *ha*, or the stems of *taro* and parts of the leaves, *'opae*, and tiny fish called *'o'opu.*

"Those are the things that the *menehune* said they like best. Oh, please work hard, Mother, so that I can leave tomorrow. I am afraid now that my father is dead, and I must find his bones and bring them back to Kipahulu."

"I too believe he is dead, son," his mother said sadly. "If he were alive, he would have found a way to send us news of him. Yes, you must find his bones. They must be buried here at Ki-pahulu, where no evil person can ask a *kahuna* to work a spell upon them. I am so glad you are a big boy now and can do this last thing for your father." She rubbed his cheek gently with her nose, the Hawaiian way of kissing.

While Laka's mother and grandmother prepared the delicacies, the boy began work on the canoe shelter. He knew he must work as fast as he could.

In the middle of the night, from the darkness above came a humming sound.

"Listen!" said Laka. "They are lifting the canoe."

Another hum, and it was halfway to the beach. A third —and there it was, in the newly-finished shelter.

"Now for the *lu'au*!" cried the little men, dancing about as they thought of all that delicious food.

Each *menehune* had a bite of *taro* leaves, one *'opae*, and one *'o'opu*.

"Now we'll get the canoe into the sea for you," they said. "In the morning you can start on your journey."

In a moment, the canoe was rocking gently on the waves. Then the little men started back to the mountains, as dawn was breaking.

"Goodby, *menehune*!" cried Laka. "And thank you!"

The hum of their voices grew fainter and farther away, and at last was heard no more.

As the sun rose from the sea, Laka sailed away in his beautifully made canoe.

3

THE PRINCESS WHO LOVED TO SURF

Kele'a's long, glistening hair lay on either cheek like the black wings of a bird. Her eyes sparkled, her skin was tanned to a golden brown because she spent so much time in the sun, and she walked like the princess that she was. She was the most beautiful young woman on the island of Maui.

Kele'a was the sister of Kawao, high chief of Maui. She lived near the beach at Hamakua-poko, and of all things in the world, she loved best to surf. Every day, crowds gathered at the shore to watch the lovely princess at her favorite sport. She was considered to be the most accomplished surf swimmer of her time.

One morning, as she swam out to catch a wave, she was surprised to see a strange canoe approaching. She stopped swimming and floated on the water for a minute, wondering what this could mean, and one of the paddlers called out: "Oh chiefess, make your landing in our canoe."

"That might be fun," she thought, and the man spoke kindly. She would try it once. She pulled herself easily into the canoe, and found it thrilling to speed swiftly toward shore with a great wave propelling the craft. Cool spray showered her bare arms and shoulders, while the morning sun was warm on her face. This was almost better than body surfing! It was different, anyway, and exciting.

Kele'a stayed aboard the canoe for several rides. Laughingly, she turned to say something to one of the paddlers, and was surprised by a crafty expression on his face. Suddenly, she felt chilled. "I'll get out now," she said. "Thank you for the rides."

But when she tried to rise, powerful arms held her—and the canoe headed for the open sea! "Let me go!" she cried, struggling. Kele'a was strong because she had done so much surfing, but she was no match for the men in the canoe. They held her fast.

Her cries were wafted back by the sea breeze to the people on the beach. "Our princess!" they cried in horror. "Kele'a!"

There was no canoe nearby in which to give chase, and by the time one had been found, the craft bearing Kele'a had vanished in the vastness of the ocean as if it had never been.

In the canoe, Kele'a regarded her captors with fear. "Where are you taking me?" she asked, forcing her voice to be steady. Whatever was going to happen to her, she would behave like a princess.

The men smiled, and they did not look unkind. "You

are fortunate," one of them said. "Our chief on O'ahu sent us to find a wife for him. We have searched the islands of Moloka'i and Lana'i, but have not found anyone worthy of our ruler, Lo Lale. At Hana we learned that the king's sister is the loveliest woman on Maui, as well as being the finest surfer. We are paying you a great honor; you will see."

Kele'a wept then. She did not want to leave her home. But what could she do? She couldn't escape from the canoe. But still, she reflected, she need not submit to the O'ahu chief. "I will not marry him," she thought defiantly. "I'll get word to my brother; he'll send for me."

The canoe landed at Wai-a-lua, and from there Kele'a was taken to where Lo Lale waited, in the forested hills above the shore. She saw that he was handsome and strong, and that he carried himself as a chief should. But when he asked her to stay with him as his wife, she told him that she could never be happy living in the hills of O'ahu.

"I want to go back to Hamakua-poko," she said. "Surfing is my life, and Maui is my home. Please send me back."

She saw that she need not send a messenger to her brother in secret, for this was a man who would respect her rank and her wishes. Lo Lale bowed before her, and told her that he would order a canoe to take her back to Maui.

He accompanied her to the beach, where she stood looking out at the mounting waves. After a few moments, Lo Lale said, "The canoe is not ready yet. Why not surf once or twice while we are waiting?"

It would be fun to try these waves! Kele'a plunged into the water and swam toward the cresting surf. Lo Lale swam strongly beside her, and together they skimmed again and again toward shore.

At last, Kele'a tired, and she sat with Lo Lale on the beach. The young chief glanced at her and said, "You see that the ocean that bounds O'ahu, too, has fine surf. If you will stay with me, you may come here every day. And sometimes, of course, I'll take you to visit your old home on Maui."

She could surf every day—and have this handsome chief for her husband, as well! But Kele'a was proud. She said with dignity, "I will stay for a time and then decide."

Lo Lale was satisfied with her answer. He had an idea that her stay would last a long time.

4

THE
POISONOUS
LIMU

At the northern end of Hale-a-ka-la there is a beautiful bay, bounded by black, jagged rocks that march into the sea as if to protect it from the ocean beyond. Here the waves sweep in toward shore in unbroken lines, and curl behind a body-surfer for a long distance before landing him on the beach. This was a favorite place for surfing long ago. The children of that time learned to swim as early as to walk, and all of the people spent much of each day in the warm blue sea.

In order to reach this bay, some of the people had to pass the house of a man named Nanaue. No one knew him very well, and all felt that there was something rather strange about him. Even on the warmest days, he wore over his shoulders a sort of cape of *lau hala* matting. No one had ever seen him without it. There was an odd-looking hump on his back, and they supposed that he wanted to conceal this.

But how could he be so vain when the days were at their hottest? The other men wore only *malo*, the briefest of garments, and they were certainly more comfortable than Nanaue.

Nanaue was a lonely sort of man, who lived by himself and seldom spoke, even to his neighbors. But sometimes, as he hoed his potato patch, he called out to those who were walking along the beach, "Where are you going?"

"Surfing," was usually the reply.

"*Pau po'o*," Nanaue said then, pointing to one of them. Or sometimes it was, "*Pau hi'u*."

And sure enough, the one to whom he had said, "*Pau po'o*," would float ashore later with his head gone. Or if it had been "*Pau hi'u*," the victim's legs were cut off as he swam.

After a time, the people began to wonder how it was that Nanaue could foretell these dreadful things. They became suspicious of him. Could he have something to do with these happenings? Perhaps the way he kept to himself made them mistrust him all the more. And it really was peculiar that he always covered the upper part of his body. He was different from other people—queer, they told each other. Sometimes they caught him with an expression on his face that struck them as sinister, and it frightened them.

"Why don't we go to see him," asked one, "and try to find out why he seems so strange—and how he knows when someone is going to be killed while swimming?"

"Good idea!" agreed another. "He's just too mysterious. Let's go!"

So a group of men went off in search of Nanaue. But when they reached his house, he wasn't there.

Outside the nearest house, a man sat repairing his fishnet.

"Where is Nanaue?" one of the men asked him.

"He's probably gone to the lava tube," the fisherman answered, nodding his head toward the end of the beach. "He's always going into that lava tube." He looked at them curiously. "What do you want him for?"

"We want to ask him how it is that he can tell when a certain person is going to lose his head or legs while swimming."

The fisherman folded his net and stood up. "I'd like to know that, too," he said. "It happened to my brother. I'll come with you."

The entrance to the lava tube was hidden by densely growing shrubs and vines. The men stood there for a moment, listening. But all they could hear was the distant plash of the sea, surging into the far end of the rocky tunnel.

"Here's the way in," said the fisherman.

He led, and the others followed. It was dark in the tunnel, which sloped downwards, but they could see a circle of bright sea and sky at its end. Nanaue was not in the tube, nor at the edge of the sea when they reached it.

"He must have gone for a swim," said one, shading his eyes and looking out over the bay. "I don't see him, though. Perhaps he has swum far out."

"We'll just have to wait until he comes in," said another.

"Perhaps we'd better hide," suggested a third. "He might be frightened off by such a large crowd waiting for him."

They concealed themselves in the foliage at the entrance to the cavern, where they could peer down the slope toward the ocean. After they had waited for what seemed a long time, a very large wave bore a figure up into the lava tube. As it stood up, they could see that the hump-backed shape was Nanaue's. Then there were scuffling sounds in the passage as he approached the landward entrance. The men leapt from their hiding places, and he saw them and began to run back toward the water.

"Catch him!" they cried, and sprang after him.

Nanaue didn't have a chance with so many men chasing him, and he was soon caught. In the struggle, his cape was torn off. There, protruding from his back, were the jaws of a shark!

A murmur went through the crowd. "A shark-man!" All of them stood gazing in horror.

It was so: on land, Nanaue was a man, but as soon as the water touched him, he became a shark. It was Nanaue himself who had been attacking people as they swam.

He was carried at once to an *imu*, or underground oven, at the edge of the bay. As one of the men was lighting a fire to heat the stones with which the pit was lined, Nanaue realized that he was going to be killed and his body put into the oven. He wriggled like a fish and slipped out of his captors' grasp, and started for the sea.

Shouting, the men dashed after him. If he reached the water, he would become a shark! Just at the edge of the

sea, one of the men caught his leg and pulled him back onto the beach. He was killed then, and his body thrown into the *imu*.

Late that afternoon, as Nanaue's body crumbled to ashes, a breeze sprang up. In a gusty swirl it caught up the ashes, still glowing, and carried them out over the bay where they were scattered upon the water. That is the end of Nanaue, the people thought with relief.

Not long afterwards, a new sort of sea-moss was noticed growing on the ocean floor. The colors in it were mingled blue, gray, and lavender, and when it was held in the sunlight it gave a shimmering, silvery effect. But though everyone loved to eat the various mosses and seaweeds found in these waters, something made them cautious about this new one. They fed it first to a hog—and the hog died.

"It is the ashes of Nanaue," they said, remembering how the charred fragments had fallen into the sea. "They have become a *limu-make*."

To this day, the silvery *limu* is poisonous and is never eaten by those who find it in the ocean of that beautiful bay.

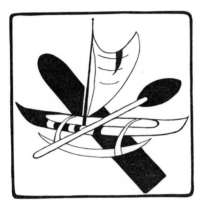

5
THE FIRST
CLOAK
OF FEATHERS

One morning King Kaka'alaneo of western Maui sent for his favorite messenger, 'Ele'io, who came in as usual on his hands and knees.

"My supply of *'awa* wine is gone," said the king, "and I want you to go to Hana today and get me some good *'awa* bushes—you know the kind I like best. Be sure you're back in time for the wine to be made from the bushes so that I can drink some of it with my dinner."

"That will be easy," said 'Ele'io. "I'll go right away."

'Ele'io was a tall young man, straight and slender as the trunk of a royal palm, and as sturdy. He was the swiftest of all the king's runners, and once he had gone all the way around the island of Maui three times in a single day.

Kings' runners, or *kukini*, were trained to take the most direct line possible: to run uphill as fast as down, to jump over boulders and streams, and to scale gulches whose sides were so steep that no plants clung to them.

'Ele'io started off confidently. He would be back from Hana before the sun had climbed to the highest point in the sky, with no trouble at all! Over a peak and through a valley of Mauna Kahalawai he ran, across the plain and along the lower slopes of the great mountain Hale-a-ka-la. It was a golden sort of day, and the sea to his left was dazzlingly blue. How nice it would be to have a swim! But no—he had better keep on, in case he should forget to come out of the water.

'Ele'io knew that the king counted on him a great deal, and sometimes he rather took advantage of his important position at court. So much depended on him as the best messenger that he felt quite secure. Still, it would be wise to get on with his errand. There would be time for a swim later.

As he ran, 'Ele'io became aware that a girl had been running ahead of him for some time, and that he had not yet caught up with her. This was strange! He saw that she was slim and graceful, and that she ran so easily that her feet seemed barely to touch the ground. She must be beautiful, a girl like that, thought 'Ele'io. I'll catch up with her and see.

He quickened his pace, but still she remained in the lead! This was preposterous! 'Ele'io ran as fast as he could, and that was as fast as the trade winds could blow. Still the girl was ahead!

They reached the end of Hale-a-ka-la and were nearing Hana, where the king's special 'awa bushes grew. But 'Ele'io couldn't stop now. He had to catch up with that girl. Around the end of the mountain she went; she seemed to fly, past Hana and into the forests of Ki-pahulu. He lost sight of her now and then among the densely growing trees, shrubs, and ferns. Then, like a wraith on the shadowed slopes, she would reappear. In a grove of *hala* trees, where long slender leaves reached down like ghostly fingers, she skimmed along as if her feet were charmed. 'Ele'io himself tripped over a root covered by fallen leaves.

Along the track over ancient lava flows, now cold and dead but rocky underfoot. On across the slopes, steep at this side of the mountain, to far Kahiki-nui.

There he caught her. She was about to enter a tower of bamboo, a *pu'o'a*, with a platform halfway up; 'Ele'io knew this was a place where the bodies of people of the higher classes were put after death.

He wasn't surprised. He had begun to suspect what this girl was. Who could run as fast as she, could keep ahead of the swiftest *kukini* for miles—who but a spirit?

She said, "You must let me go, for this is where I live."

But still he held her, not wanting to let such a beautiful spirit go.

"Oh, please!" she cried. "I must go, really. But if you will find my parents' home and tell them that I sent you, they will give you a cloak made of feathers."

A cloak made of feathers! Never had 'Ele'io heard of such a thing. Slowly he released her, and stood watching as she disappeared into the *pu'o'a*. A plan was beginning to form in his mind.

He had studied the art of *po'i 'uhane*, spirit entrapping, with an old priest of the king's. He knew it was because of

this knowledge that he had been able to see the girl's spirit, which would be invisible to most people. Perhaps he could bring her back to life. . . .

He climbed to the platform of the *pu'o'a*, where the girl's body was lying, and gazed down at her for a long time. "It'll make me late with the king's *'awa*," he thought. "But still, I must do what I can for this girl. She is so beautiful! And am I not the favorite *kukini*? Surely the king will forgive me."

He found the girl's parents very sad, and wailing as was the custom after a death. They stopped when they heard what 'Ele'io proposed to do.

"First call in your relatives," he said, "and ask them to help you to build a *lanai* with an altar at one end."

This was done, and the *lanai* was decorated in *lei* of *'ie'ie* vines and fragrant *maile*, with ferns and sweet-smelling ginger. 'Ele'io ordered a hog to be cooked, and red and white fish, and cocks of red, black, and white. These were placed on the altar with bananas of the kind used in sacrifice to the gods.

Then he asked for a period of prayer, during which no sound must be heard. The muzzles of dogs and pigs had to be tied, and chickens placed under calabashes so they would think night had fallen and would be quiet. All of the people were to pray to their gods.

'Ele'io then ran with all speed the many miles back to Hana, where he found some *'awa* bushes of the kind used by priests. With the plants in his hand, he remembered the errand on which he had been sent. A doubt came into his mind, but he thrust it aside.

He returned to Kahiki-nui, and when the 'awa wine was made and all was ready, he offered it with the food to the gods and asked their help. The girl's spirit had come to hover near him, though it couldn't be seen by the other men, not even by her father. He grasped the spirit now and ran with it to the pu'o'a, where he thrust it into the girl's body. For a long moment he waited, scarcely daring to breathe. Then she moved, smiled at him, and he could see that she was a mortal girl again.

Her father was so grateful that he asked 'Ele'io to remain and to marry his daughter.

But 'Ele'io said, "She is so beautiful that she ought to be a queen. Let me take her to Kaka'alaneo, whose court lies beyond two mountains."

The next day 'Ele'io and the girl, Kanikania'ula, started out on the long journey, bearing the feather cloak as a gift for the king, and the wine that was left from the ceremony. They had to go more slowly this time, for the girl could not travel so swiftly as her spirit had done.

When at last they had rounded the one mountain and crossed the other, 'Ele'io said, "Wait here until sundown. If I'm not back, you will know that I am dead and you must go back." He had begun to fear that the king might be angry even with his favorite messenger.

As he approached La-haina he saw a gathering of men, and in the still, bright air, waves of heat shimmered as they rose from the ground. 'Ele'io realized that an imu, an underground oven, had been made, and that he was to be killed and his body burned in it. This was the fate of those who disobeyed the king.

When the men fell upon him, he cried, "Let me see my master once more, and die in his presence!"

"We have our orders," said the leader. "You are to be killed right here," and he raised a heavy club.

"I have brought him a gift," said 'Ele'io, "so fabulous you won't believe it. A cloak made of feathers! I want to give it to him myself, before I die." He did not speak of the girl who, to his mind, should be queen. He would tell only the king of her—if he were allowed to live long enough.

A cloak made of feathers! None of the men had ever seen or heard of such a thing.

"Let's let him make his gift," suggested one. "We can follow, and be ready to kill him afterwards." 'Ele'io was, after all, a great favorite.

"Well—all right," agreed the leader, lowering his club. "Straight to the king now, and we'll all be right behind you."

'Ele'io went in to the king's presence on hands and knees.

The king, infuriated, cried, "Why are you still alive?"

'Ele'io said quickly, "Hear me, O king. It is in my power to make your name famous."

He unwrapped the cloak and laid it before Kaka'alaneo, who was enchanted. He had never dreamed of a cloak made of feathers.

'Ele'io said, "And I have even greater beauty to show you, sire. May I do so?"

"Yes, go," said the king, still examining the beautiful red and yellow feathers and the way they were woven intricately to make a cloak. How fine he would look in this!

When 'Ele'io returned with Kanikania'ula, the king forgave his messenger completely.

"You will be my queen," he said to the girl. And instead of drinking the wine, he offered it to his gods in thanks.

As for 'Ele'io, he became a greater favorite now than ever before. And from that time on, feather cloaks, or *ahu'ula,* were made for royalty and the high *ali'i* alone. No commoner might wear one.

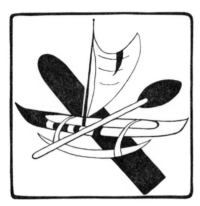

6

THE
MISCHIEF-
MAKER

Kaulula'au's father looked at the young sweet potato plants that had been pulled up, and frowned.

"Kaulu!" he called. "Come here, please." When the boy stood before him, he asked, "Who did this?"

"Who could have done such a thing?" said the boy innocently. He smiled a little to himself, and his father looked at him sternly.

Kaulula'au was the son of the great king, Kaka'alaneo, who ruled that part of Maui that looks toward the setting sun, and of beautiful Queen Kanikania'ula. Kaka'alaneo had tried always to be good and kind to the boy. He had had all the children of his district who had been born on the same day as Kaulula'au brought to live at court, to be playmates for his son. "Perhaps I have been *too* kind," he thought now. "Kaulu needs a firmer hand than he has been accustomed to."

"You know, Kaulu," he said, "that you are a chief, and

we *ali'i* do not do such things. I am not blaming your playmates, for it is you who are the chief among them. You are a leader, I can see that. But you must learn to be a leader for good, not for mischief."

The boy started to protest, but his father held up a silencing hand. "I know you did this, Kaulu, and I was hoping you would tell me so yourself. You've always been fond of playing tricks on people, and you are teaching your friends to play them with you. Tricks that don't hurt anyone are one thing, but this—don't you realize that food is very important, and that the gods don't like to see it destroyed?"

"Yes, Father, I know that's true," said Kaulula'au. "I'll try to be better."

But tricks and mischief-making were a part of the boy's nature, and he just couldn't seem to help playing pranks and getting his friends to help. Before long, his father found some young banana trees uprooted. And then, a whole grove of just-planted breadfruit trees!

This time, Kaka'alaneo was really angry. "I'm warning you, Kaulu," he said. "This sort of thing can't go on. If it doesn't stop . . ." He left the threat unspoken.

For some time, Kaulula'au was able to restrain himself and just played some tricks on his friends that were really funny and did not harm. But one night, as he walked along the shore, he passed his father's fleet of canoes beached there. He thought, "Wouldn't it be fun to . . . ?"

In the morning, a messenger ran to the king with the news that the canoes were missing.

"The canoes missing!" cried the king. "What on earth

could have happened to them?" Then a look of understanding came into his face, and his expression changed. "Send Kaulula'au to me!" he thundered.

When the boy came, his father said in a controlled voice, "Kaulu, tell me what you know about the missing fleet of canoes."

Kaulula'au looked out over the white-capped sea to the island of Lana'i. "You know, Father, there are said to be evil spirits, *akua lapu*, on Lana'i. Perhaps they had something to do with it." He glanced sideways at his father, to see how he was taking this.

Kaka'alaneo looked across the channel to the mountains of Lana'i, rising from the sea. "That gives me an idea," he said slowly. "I know that you and your friends pulled the canoes to the edge of the water, so they would float away when the tide rose." He paused, and the boy wondered what was coming next.

"When something like this happens again," the chief said, "I'm going to send you to Lana'i. Perhaps you'll be able to trick those evil spirits!"

Kaulula'au didn't want at all to have this happen. He looked fearfully toward the other island, so beautiful yet said to be peopled with unknown terrors. But then he thought, "My father wouldn't really send me there. He's just trying to frighten me."

Not long afterward, it was discovered that someone had stolen into the sacred temple by night, and painted in rainbow hues the pure white birds that awaited sacrificial rites there.

Calling his son to him, Kaka'alaneo said, "The time has come for you to go." He looked at the boy with sorrowful eyes, but did not relent. "You may say goodby to your mother, while I call for a canoe to take you."

"Take me—where, Father?" faltered Kaulula'au.

"Don't you remember? To Lana'i, of course."

So he was really to go to the island where the *akua lapu* lived! He went to Kanikania'ula to tell her the news, and she begged her husband to change his mind. "Those spirits will kill Kaulu!" she cried, clutching her son to her.

But the king said, "I warned him fairly, and he must go. The canoe is ready, son, with paddlers who will leave you there."

So he really had to go. . . . Well, in that case, there was only one thing to do. Kaulula'au straightened his shoulders and stood stalwartly before his father. "That is true," he said. "You warned me fairly. But I'm going to do my best to outwit those spirits. A year from tonight, look across the channel to that headland that you see. If a fire burns there, you will know that I have succeeded. Otherwise . . ."

"Otherwise," said the king gravely, "you will be dead. I shall look for the fire, my son."

Kaulula'au stood alone on the beach of Lana'i, watching as the canoe that had brought him there became a small speck on the waves, and finally vanished in the distance toward his beloved Maui.

He looked about him with apprehension. No living

person was on the island, he had been told; it was inhabited only by evil spirits. Where were they? Did they know he was here? Well, there wasn't time to waste pondering this. He had much to do. First, look for water.

He went up the hillside, through a grove of *hala* trees whose long slender leaves rustled in the sea breeze. "It's like people whispering," he thought, glancing over his shoulder, "or the *akua*!" He hurried on.

Above the grove he found what he wanted, a spring of mountain water. He splashed some over his face and it was lovely and cool. As the ripples he had caused subsided, he could see his reflection staring back at him. A good sturdy boy, the eyes alert and watchful—he should be able to match wits with anyone.

Now for breadfruit, *taro*, bananas. And a place to sleep. When he came across a little cave, its entrance nearly hidden by hanging vines, he stored in it the *lau hala* mat, *tapa* blankets, fishing lines, net, and food that he had brought with him in the canoe. Then when he had found fruit and vegetables for the future, he went back toward the sea to look for a good fishing spot.

Here it was cliffy, and as he rounded some rocks he saw a band of about ten people. People? He looked more closely. There was something odd about them, a shifty sort of look; something strange that he didn't like.

"Aloha," he said politely, and they responded.

"Have you come here to live?" one of them asked.

"If I like it well enough," Kaulula'au replied cautiously.

"And where do you plan to sleep tonight?" another asked.

Something warned him not to speak of his cave. "In that patch of reeds, I think," he said. "It should be comfortable there."

When night fell, he lay in the patch of reeds, not intending to stay. But he was so tired after the day's activity that he fell asleep. Suddenly, a god spoke to him in his dreams and said, "Quick! Run for your cave."

Kaulula'au went as quickly and quietly as he could, and slept well. In the morning, he saw that the patch of reeds had been trampled flat.

When he met the band of strange beings shortly afterward, they looked as if they couldn't believe their eyes. "Where did you sleep?" one of them gasped.

"Didn't you see me settling myself in the patch of reeds? I dreamed I heard someone walking through them."

"And where will you be tonight?" There was a wicked look in the eyes of the one who put this question, and Kaulula'au took care with his answer. These were indeed the *akua lapu*, he realized.

"I passed through a grove of *hala*," he said, "and just at this side there is a fine big tree. I thought of what a good sleeping place it would make."

"Oh, yes!" all of the spirits agreed at once. "That's an excellent place! Well, have a good night." They passed on their way.

Kaulula'au spent some time fishing in a cove he had found, then went back to his cave, had some food and walked down to settle himself among the branches of the big *hala* tree he had described. I know they are watching from somewhere, he thought, yawning and stretching and trying to behave like a boy who would soon be asleep. The tree was, in fact, quite comfortable, and he wished he could stay there all night. But he had other plans.

After a time, he became conscious again of the whispering leaves—or voices. I can't risk staying here any longer, he thought.

It was so dark now that the *hala* trees about him were only formless shapes in the night. He slid silently from the tree. In daylight his courage had been high, but now he moved stealthily, straining his eyes as he peered into the night. Perhaps the *akua lapu* could see in the dark! But still, they had missed his move the night before.

He skirted the grove as quietly as he could, staying close to its protecting blackness. But before he was able to run for the cave, he heard a great commotion in the tree he had just left. It sounded as if the *akua* were beating its branches with clubs. He pulled himself into a tree at the far side, and listened, shivering.

In the morning, Kaulula'au took *poi* and fish from his cave to the spring. He was eating there when several of the *akua* appeared. They gazed at him in amazement.

"Aloha," he said. "I had a good night's sleep. I hope you did."

"Where were you?" asked one of the spirits.

"Don't you remember? I slept in a tree. I had another strange dream—as if someone were tapping at the branches with twigs."

"Will you sleep there tonight?"

"Mm . . . I don't know. I saw a nice big cave away up the hillside. It would be comfortable to lie down."

That evening he took some grass into the big cave, as if he were going to make a bed. When it was dark, he stole across the slope to the little cave where he had hidden his belongings. "I must be careful every night to get here in time," he thought. "I had a narrow escape last night!"

The next morning he walked up to the big cave and saw that it was full of stones. "The *akua lapu* must have thrown them in an effort to kill me," he thought. "Well, I'd like to kill *them*. Lana'i would be a lovely island if it weren't for those old evil spirits."

When he met them, he told them that he had dreamed some leaves fell on him during the night.

Every night now, the *akua lapu* made some attempt to do away with the boy. But Kaulula'au's practice in tricks came to his rescue, time after time. He had to be alert always, but each time he outwitted his enemies.

He began at last to see that this was having an effect on them. As the months wore on, they became very nervous —and one day, one of them died.

"Ha! The first one!" thought the boy. "Others will follow."

By day, the spirits continued to appear friendly, but towards evening each night, one of them inquired where the boy planned to sleep.

One time he replied, "In that patch of thorny vines. I think I can get under the thorns, and it will be protected and quite comfortable."

The next morning, the spirits were all badly scratched; two of them so badly that they became swollen and died. Perhaps the thorns are poisonous, Kaulula'au thought.

Another time his reply to the nightly query was, "I'll sleep in the large surf that rolls as high as a house."

Three of the spirits became exhausted in the surf, and drowned.

"More than half the band is gone now!" thought Kaulula'au exultingly. And those who were left, all but their chief, were becoming more and more nervous and tired from loss of sleep. One of them drowned even in the small surf.

Kaulula'au himself slept soundly each night. He did not again make the mistake of waiting so long that he had to sleep in a tree, or some other uncomfortable place. And he kept the spirits so busy that they had no time, nor energy, to find his cave.

At last, only the chief of the spirits was left. He was the most dangerous of all, the boy knew. But he had been thinking about the possibility of having to deal with this one in the end, and he had a scheme. The year was over now, and his parents would be watching for his fire.

He went to the spring and climbed a tree that hung over the water, taking with him a heavy stone. There he lay along one of the branches, and waited.

When the chief came and knelt beside the spring to drink, he saw Kaulula'au's face reflected in the water. Immediately, the boy made a hideous grimace.

Thinking his enemy was in the spring, the chief jumped in—and Kaulula'au let the stone fall on him.

The chief was hurt but not killed, and he was frightened out of his senses. With a cry, he climbed out of the spring and ran at top speed down the hillside. From a cliff he

The Mischief-maker ‡ 51

dived into the sea, and swam as fast as he could away from Lana'i.

"That spirit will never return to this island," said the boy to himself as he watched. "And just in time! My year is up."

Joyfully, he gathered wood for his fire, and took a branch from a *hau* tree and one from a sandalwood, and rubbed them together until sparks came. He watched as the flames caught the dry branches, and smoke began to curl upward. All day he fed the fire with more and more wood, until in the darkness it was a leaping, roaring beacon that would be seen across the channel on Maui.

"Maui!" thought Kaulula'au. "Will my father let me return now?"

As the first light streaked the ocean, the boy saw a canoe approaching. He stood gazing as it skimmed closer and closer. Could it be? Yes! Only his father stood so tall, so erect and powerful!

"Father!" he cried as the king reached shore. "The *akua lapu* are all gone now. May I come home?"

"Yes, son," said Kaka'alaneo. "Your friends have missed you, and so have your mother and I. I know that you have learned your lesson, and you've done a fine thing to get rid of the *akua lapu*."

"Lana'i is a wonderful island," said the boy. "People must come to live here now. But as for me, I want to go home to Maui!"

7

KUʻULA, THE FISHERMAN

Kuʻula was a man who loved to fish. He lived on the eastern shore of the island of Maui, where the sun rises from the sea and casts a pathway of gold upon the water. Sometimes at daybreak he would stand on the beach and think, "All the ocean in front of my house, all that I can see out to the very edge where sea meets sky, is mine." He was grateful for this, and happy with his lot in life—a fine family, the sea that he loved, and the opportunity to spend most of his time fishing.

Often he gave thanks to the god of fishing, as he took his canoe and paddled out over the shining water or as he fished from shore, walking out onto a rocky promontory with his net in folds over his shoulder.

On these days his sharp eyes gazed into the sea until he saw a school of fish, and then he threw his net so that it spread wide over the water, and drew it toward him with the fish he had snared. Usually his son ʻAiʻai went with him, for he wanted to learn to be a great fisherman like his father.

One day as Kuʻula was walking over the rocks with his net, he thought, "It would be nice to have a fishpond right in front of my house. I believe I could get all the best fish to come into it by giving the god of fishing an offering each day of the first fish that I catch."

"'Aiʻai," he said, "I want to make a wall of rocks in the sea, for a fishpond. Will you help me?"

"Of course, but how will you get the fish into it?"

"There will be enough space for very small fish to come into the pond, and for sea water to flow in and out. We'll feed the fish *taro,* and soon they'll be too big to swim out again."

"What a good idea!" 'Aiʻai said. "Let's start right away."

When the pond was finished, Kuʻula built a shrine of coral on the rocky shore above it, just where the sandy beach met the promontory that edged his bay. The shrine was a sort of altar on which he could lay his offerings to the god of fishing.

Kuʻula's neighbors soon began to notice that he caught more fish than any of the other fishermen. They watched with interest as, each morning, he took his first catch to the altar of coral. There must be something to Kuʻula's idea of making offerings of fish, they thought.

One day, as Kuʻula was hauling in a full net, one of King Kamohoaliʻi's *kukini* came running up to him. "Come quickly!" the messenger cried. "The king wants to see you right away."

"Good Heavens!" thought Ku'ula, so excited that he dropped his net into the fishpond and the fish swarmed out of it. What could the great king want? Trembling, he went at once to Ka-'uiki Hill, where the palace stood. The palace was a group of grass houses that were larger than the usual home of a chief.

Ku'ula went before his ruler rather shakily, on his hands and knees, and waited for the great man to speak.

"Ku'ula, I have heard that you are a good fisherman," Kamohoali'i said.

"I don't forget the god of fishing, O king," Ku'ula replied in a low voice. "And he rewards me."

"Good," said the king. "Very good. I now appoint you my head fisherman."

"O, my king!" stammered Ku'ula, unable to believe his ears.

"But don't forget," cautioned the monarch, "that I shall expect you to provide me with the best fish of each season."

"I will do my best," promised Ku'ula. There had been no need to be afraid, after all! He felt sure that he could do as the king had bidden. Filled with relief, and with pride at the honor bestowed upon him, he went back to search for his net and to catch some fish for the king.

For many years Ku'ula was able to fulfill all of the king's wishes, and he became famous as the best fisherman on the island. Others began to build shrines too, and called them *ku'ula* after the man who had made the first one.

But finally Ku'ula began to notice that there were fewer and fewer fish in his pond. He couldn't understand

it. Had he done something to anger the god of fishing? This was serious, for if he couldn't catch as many fish as the king wanted, something dreadful would surely happen to him. The king was extremely fond of fish, and very particular. Ku'ula resolved to watch his pond night and day, with 'Ai'ai's help, until he found out why the fish were no longer in it.

For a time they saw no reason for it and became greatly discouraged. At last, there were practically no fish at all left in the pond. Ku'ula didn't like to think what might happen to him now.

The next morning he rose early to relieve 'Ai'ai at his watch; and just at dawn, the two could make out the sinuous form of a huge *puhi* swimming under the sparkling water of the pond. The great creature slithered over the wall and out of the fishpond.

"That old eel!" thought Ku'ula furiously. "He has been helping himself to my fish at night, when we haven't been able to spy him."

"That must be Ko'ona," a neighbor said. "The people of Moloka'i won't like that, because he is the guardian of many of them."

"He's the guardian of some of us, too," said another. "Let him come and live near us for a while."

But most of the people were afraid when they now began to see the eel slinking through the sea or lying in great, slimy coils on the rocks. He was thirty feet long!

"He'll go to live in Kapuka-ulua," Ku'ula said, "the Cave of the Ulua Fish."

The others knew that Ku'ula was wise in the ways of the

inhabitants of the ocean, and that he must be right. The cave was far out to sea, at the bottom of the ocean.

"Maybe he'll stay out there," said someone.

But Ku'ula shook his head. "Not he. That one gets around." And *into my own fishpond!* he added in his thoughts.

He would have to be caught, that was all there was to it. Ku'ula was growing old now, and he asked his son if he would take charge of catching the eel.

"I'd be glad to," replied 'Ai'ai, who by now had grown into young manhood. "There's nothing I'd like better. And I'll get him, wait and see!" He was eager to hunt out the monster. It was now or never, he knew, for the king's head fisherman—the father whom 'Ai'ai loved.

He called together all the men who feared Ko'ona and told them of his plan to surround the creature when he glided up onto the rocks to sun himself, as he did now and then.

But when they attempted to do this, they saw a man running toward the eel. He was going to warn him!

"Hurry!" cried 'Ai'ai to the others. "*Wikiwiki!*" But they were too late, and Ko'ona slid back into the water.

Ku'ula shook his head sadly, and his son noticed that the father's shoulders were drooping like those of an old man. "I must do something to help him," 'Ai'ai thought. "I must hit upon another scheme."

After thinking as hard as he could for a long time, he asked the men whom he knew he could trust if they would make two long ropes of the bark of the *hau* tree. When they were done, 'Ai'ai took a *hokeo* in which he placed a very large hook; then he split a coconut with an adze and found two heavy stones.

One of the ropes, the gourd with the hook, the coconut and stones went into his canoe. He took the other rope to a canoe of the next beach, and said, "Now let's go out in these two canoes and find that *puhi*."

The men paddled far, far out into the ocean. At last 'Ai'ai said, "Here is the place. I'll dive down to take a look around."

He stared into the depths of the waters. How far below the surface the cave must be! Well, he'd better get it over with. It was up to him to save his father from the king's wrath.

Taking one of the stones in his hands, he dived in. Down, down he went, carried by the weight of the stone —past clumps of seaweed, schools of fish, down through the shining water, which grew darker as he sank farther. At last, the ocean floor!

Before him was a large cave, and in the dimly glowing undersea light, he saw many *ulua* swimming around in an excited way at the entrance. Surely, Ko'ona must be near! The *ulua* were frightened. "Poor things," thought 'Ai'ai, "they have lost their home in the cave, and the eel must have eaten a great many of them." He let go of the stone and rose to the surface. He had found the monster's lair.

Could he be sure that the men would not waver in the task of conquering Ko'ona? "I'll appeal to their pride," he thought, and said, "Now, let's have a contest! We'll see which canoe can pull that old *puhi* ashore."

He tied the huge hook to the *hau* bark rope of each

canoe, baited it with pieces of coconut and, holding it and the second stone in his arms, sank again to the mouth of the cave. Placing the hook there, he said a quick prayer in the name of his parents, and ascended once more.

Then began the waiting and watching. Surely the gods, especially the god of fishing, would be kind to his father, 'Ai'ai thought. That deity must know that Ku'ula had come to the end of his supply of fish for the king. Wouldn't he help now? 'Ai'ai sat praying to him, and watching the ropes. One of these lines he held in his hands.

As time went on, and the canoes rose and fell gently with the currents of the ocean but the lines hung inert, some of the men became restless.

"It's getting late," one said, "and we're a long way from home. What's the sense in waiting any longer?"

"Yes, let's go home," agreed another. "That eel is too smart to let himself be caught."

The men grumbled a bit, but couldn't seem to make up their minds about what to do. Some wanted to go, others were willing to wait, and they quarreled a little.

'Ai'ai was worried. He closed his eyes and prayed very hard. All at once he felt a slight tug on the rope he was holding. He sat tense, waiting for it to come again. There it was, stronger than before!

"We've got him!" he shouted.

Ko'ona had been fooled by the coconut and was caught on the hook! The men of both canoes paddled with all their might, glad now that they had waited and were having this contest. Looking back, 'Ai'ai could see the monstrous eel streaking through the water at the end of the two lines, thrashing his tail but unable to free himself. The canoes rocked with the force of his struggles.

"Each canoe to its own beach!" called 'Ai'ai. "We'll see now which team can drag Ko'ona up onto the shore."

He himself swam in when they neared the beach and hurried to the top of the hill Na-iwi-o-Pele to watch. From there he saw the men of his canoe win. The huge creature was landed!

But try as they might, no one was able to kill him.

"Come and help us!" the men cried to 'Ai'ai.

'Ai'ai scrambled down the rocky hillside. It was up to him now. What should he do? He picked up three *pohaku 'ala*; he was strong, and good at throwing. He hurled the first of these stones at the great tossing body, and the second. Still Ko'ona twisted about on the beach in a violent effort to free himself from the hook.

The third and last stone. . . . 'Ai'ai said a swift prayer, and threw it straight at the eel's head. After a last quiver, the great creature lay dead.

When the others had gone, 'Ai'ai stood beside the pond with his father, watching for the fish to return to it. It wasn't long before they began to come again—all but the *ulua*, who stayed to enjoy the freedom of their cave, Kapuka-ulua, now that their enemy Ko'ona was no more.

As for Ku'ula, now that he was assured of fish to supply Kamohoali'i, he stood straight and tall again as he hauled in his net. It made 'Ai'ai happy to see him.

Ku'ula himself is now the god of fishing. And the body of Ko'ona, a thirty-foot stony ridge, can still be seen where 'Ai'ai killed him.

8

KA-MALO
AND THE
SHARK GOD

The people of Mapulehu Valley on Moloka'i were dismayed to hear the beat of the sacred drums of Kupa issuing from within the king's *heiau*. They knew that the great *ali'i* had gone off on a fishing excursion, but even had they not known this, they would have been aware that it was not Kupa himself who struck the drums that day.

Fear swept through the valley as if borne inland by the sea breeze. Never before had anyone but the king drummed upon these instruments dedicated to his sole use. Who could it be? The strokes were amateurish, not like the practiced ones of the king, who was so skilled that he could speak through his rhythm to his priests.

The *heiau* of 'Ili'ili-'opae was the largest temple in all the Islands, and Kupa lived within its walls. The people crept toward it now, none daring to approach too closely, but wanting to see who should emerge before the king's return. Drumbeats throbbed through the valley and vibrated from its cliffs; then, all at once, they were stilled. The watchers knew that now was the time. . . .

They might have guessed! Swiftly, silently, two small forms slipped through the gate and vanished among the trees so quickly that they might have been apparitions.

"Ka-malo's boys!" sounded like a breath stirring from one to another. "The sons of the *kahuna*!" Awed, they knew the sure fate in store for the culprits, even though their father was the king's own priest.

The boys ran like flying shadows to their house beside the sea. They were a little frightened by what they had done —yet, what fun it had been! What a sense of power they had had, as the tones reverberated about the valley!

All the same, they looked at one another uncertainly. "Shall we swim?" suggested one.

In a moment they were in the water. Here they felt safe, at home, and soon they forgot the fear that had been a part of the excitement of the prank, but which had mounted to panic as they fled the *heiau*.

How beautiful was this bay, and their valley! Sheer ridges rose above the sea as though sculptured by the hand of a Polynesian god. Now, near the end of day, the channel was an expanse of dark blue with white-capped ripples, and beyond, the peaks of Mauna Kahalawai on Maui seemed very close.

"Some day we'll swim right across the channel and see if the valleys of Maui can be as lovely as our own," they said.

Some day. . . . Life seemed to stretch limitlessly before them.

But there was to be no "some day" for these boys. On Kupa's return, his people told him what had happened—how dared they not tell?—and the king ordered that the boys be put to death.

Sick with despair, Ka-malo went to the *ali'i* to plead for his sons. "They are little more than children, sire," he said. "They are mischievous, not really bad."

But Kupa would not forgive. His sacred drums had been violated; the boys must die.

Heartbroken, the priest vowed to devote his life to revenge his sons' deaths. He traveled in turn to each of the *kahuna nui*, the high priests, of the island to ask for aid. But all were in such terror of the wrath of Kupa that they feared to help him. Bone-weary after long futile months, Ka-malo took the only course left to him. He sought out the home of the dreaded shark god, Kauhuhu.

Carrying a black pig over his shoulders as an offering, he made his way across a mountainous part of the island and down the *pali* to Ka-laupapa. Here the shark god's *heiau* was situated, and its priest told Ka-malo where he would find the cave in which Kauhuhu lived.

Near exhaustion, Ka-malo proceeded. The pig on his shoulders seemed very heavy now, and he stumbled over the lava rock as he rounded the foot of the cliffs to the great cavern, Ana'opuhi, the Cave of the Eel.

It was lucky for him that the god was not there. The dragons Waka and Mo'o shouted warnings to him. "Keep away!" they cried. "This cave is *kapu*—no one is allowed to enter here." These were the *kahu*, the caretakers, of Kauhuhu. Something in Ka-malo's appearance must have

appealed to them, or they would have captured him for their master's dinner.

Ka-malo answered, "It matters little whether I live or die, unless I can avenge the deaths of my sons." He told the dragons what had happened and they listened with sympathy.

"We will hide you," said Waka and Mo'o. "Here, see, under this pile of *kalo* peelings." Quickly they buried him and the pig, leaving only enough space so that Ka-malo could see the ocean. "Watch as the sea rises," they said. "The waves will roll in higher and higher, and then eight huge ones will wash onto the beach. On the eighth will come our god, Kauhuhu. Then lie as still as if you were dead, for that is what you will be if he discovers you too soon—and we will be too."

Ka-malo lay looking out over the swelling sea and listening to the crash of surf against the cliffs, and he thought of his boys and of how they had loved to swim in the ocean in all its moods. At length there came a wave so large that he knew it to be the first of the eight. As each receded and the next rose yet higher, he counted. The sixth, the seventh—and finally one that swept right up into the cave.

As the water swirled and eddied back into the sea, Kauhuhu appeared—a man. When on land, he took the form of a man always; in the sea, he was a shark.

"Who is here?" he thundered. "I smell a stranger in my cave!" He searched about, but ignored the familiar heap of *kalo* peelings. Ka-malo might have gone undetected, had not the pig squealed.

Kauhuhu caught the priest from his hiding place and furiously raised him to his great jaw.

But Ka-malo cried, "E Kauhuhu! Hear me first. Then, if you will, eat me."

Kauhuhu was surprised into putting the priest down, and quickly Ka-malo told his tale. Then he offered the black pig to the god.

Although greatly feared, Kauhuhu was, like other gods and men, a mixture of good and bad. He felt that Kupa had been overly severe in taking the boys' lives, and agreed to help their unhappy father.

Ka-malo's instructions were to carry the shark god's priest on his back up the cliffs of Ka-laupapa and across the mountains to Ka-malo's own *heiau*. There the two priests were to build a *kapu* fence around it and to raise the *kapu* flags of white *kapa*. In the enclosure they must gather together black pigs by the *lau*—four hundred, a sacred number—and procure red fish and white chickens in equal quantity.

"Wait then," Kauhuhu said, "for I will come. One day you will see a small cloud over the island of Lana'i, as white as the snows of Hale-a-ka-la but no larger than a man's hand. As it floats across the channel, against the wind, it will grow until it covers the peaks of Mapulehu Valley. A rainbow will arch overhead, and the people will think, How beautiful! But not for long. . . . Now, go."

Ka-malo scarcely felt the weight of the shark god's priest on the journey, and with new vigor he attacked the problems of a *kapu* fence for his temple and collected the offering. Each day he watched the skies toward Lana'i.

At last! A tiny cloud drifted across Kalohi Channel against the wind, growing as it approached until it overhung the peaks above the valley. The people wondered about this strange cloud, and when they saw the glorious rainbow they stood marveling. An unearthly atmosphere hovered about the place, as though cloud and rainbow presaged some supernatural event.

And so it was. A sudden wind arose, black clouds massed, thunder cracked and lightning streaked across the sky. Rain fell in such torrents that Kupa and his people were swept into the bay, where they were eaten by Kauhuhu and his shark friends.

All, that is, except Ka-malo and his family, and Kauhuhu's priest. The storm never touched the walls of the *heiau*.

After this the bay was called 'Ai-Kanaka, The Place of the Man-eaters. It is said that even now when the mountains are capped by great clouds and a rainbow arches over this valley, thunderous wind and rain storms will follow.

9

GLISTENING
WATERS

Popoʻalaea sat at the top of the cliff Pali-ku. Hale-a-ka-la Crater lay like a giant tapestry before her, stretching from the fertile region just below, out across lava rock and volcanic sands with their ancient cinder cones, to the far distant rim. Behind her, Ki-pahulu Valley was a chasm that plunged to the sea, its ridged walls forested with *koa*, *ʻohiʻa-lehua*, and the big-leafed shrub *ʻapeʻape*.

That day, as so often, the princess was watching the *koaʻe-kea* as they glided lightly through the air. "How graceful they are," she thought, "and how free."

Free! Oh, the glory it would be, to be as free as these white-tailed birds who flew out over the sea, then back to dip and swerve about the cliff before landing at their flocking-place near Kau-po Gap. They were so accustomed to the girl's presence that they seemed not to fear her, and sometimes skimmed in close to the silent, motionless figure. Now and then one would perch quite near her.

How near—and yet how far! Theirs was the freedom of the air, of all that she could see—crater, descending mountain and valley, and expanse of sea. And hers—tears filled her eyes as she contemplated her lot.

The chief Makea had won the hand of lovely Popoʻalaea in games of skill and strength-testing, and had brought her to this far place, where she became known as the Princess of Pali-ku. Every day she climbed the face of the cliff by a pathway that she knew, and watched the birds come and go. It was lonely here, which was just what Makea wanted for his beautiful young wife.

He was fiercely jealous, and had built their home far up on the mountain slopes, near the gap in the crater's wall. His desire was to keep her from the eyes of all other men, especially (she knew), of the brother who was so dear to her heart; that deeply loved younger brother who lived at such a distance from her, on the far side of the mountain beyond Hana.

She feared Makea, and his rages and great strength. There were times when he had threatened to kill her because of his unreasoning jealousy. Oh, why could she not be as one of the sea-birds and soar aloft, away from the power of the husband she did not love? For the first time she thought: "Must I always be a prisoner?"

Quickly, before she could lose courage at the audacity of this idea, she ran down the pathway, slipping and sliding, caring not that she tore her *tapa* dress and skinned her ankles and elbows. She hurried through the tall, damp grass and ferns that grew under *mamane* trees, and *ʻohiʻa* with its *lehua* blossoms like feathery red birds.

All the way to the Gap and along the rocky trail to her home, she was thinking rapidly. Makea was away on one of his frequent trips. One of the princess's attendants was a girl of about her own age, and always Popoʻalaea had seen kindness in her eyes, and sympathy, as if she were sorry that the tyranny of Makea kept his young wife apart from all except those who served her—and himself.

The girl was walking from one of the thatched houses to another, and Popoʻalaea beckoned to her. Startled, with downcast eyes, she came.

"I must speak with you, Ululani," Popoʻalaea said softly. "See that it is you alone who stands with my *kahili*, while I sit this evening watching the sun sink below the crater's rim."

Ululani was able to manage this. As Popoʻalaea saw the shadows of the volcanic cones lengthen toward her, and their sands change from pale to deep rose, she murmured constantly. The girl holding the feathered standard stood behind her, still as a statue, all of her attention focused on what the princess was saying.

Popoʻalaea had made her plan. She would steal from her sleeping house and meet Ululani, and by darkness they would start traveling toward the home of the princess's brother.

"O, my princess," faltered the girl. "Do you dare? What if—what if—"

Popoʻalaea knew that she was thinking, "What if Makea should return?" She looked up into the frightened face of her attendant.

"I dare," she said. "And you?"

Ululani bowed her head and spoke in a low voice. "Anything," she said. "Anything for you, *E ke kamali'i wahine.*" She knew that this could mean death for her, as well as for Popo'alaea.

The two fled, silent and ethereal as ghosts, before the moon rose. Ululani carried the princess's own *kahili* and some lengths of *tapa* with which to cover themselves when they found a resting place.

They cut across the mountain in the direction of Kipahulu, not daring to take the lower trail of King Kamohoali'i's *kukini* that led to Hana and beyond. The danger of running into one of these messengers was too great. Instead, they crossed the deep valleys as best they could, and traveled by underground passages much of the way. These were ancient lava tubes, so eerie that the girls did not venture far along them by night.

Usually they were lucky enough to find a cave that offered some small protection from the dampness, and here they would roll themselves in *tapa* for the night. Each day they walked as far as they could, coming out into the sunlight briefly to find berries and other fruit on which to survive.

At last, the princess's brother's house! They approached it cautiously in the early evening, and sister and brother were joyful at being reunited.

"But sister, you must not stay," he said. "Makea will surely think of seeking you here. We must find you a hiding place until—until—"

"Until when, brother?"

He held her at arms' length and regarded her sadly. "There is only one course I can think of that will save you. When the opportunity comes, you must go by canoe to another island."

"For how long?" she asked through sudden tears.

He clasped her to him and said, "Forever."

I knew it would be so, she thought. I have always known, really, the true meaning of my name. Most people thought that Popoʻalaea meant "Ball of red clay." But there were those who said its real translation was "A ball rolling and seeking tomorrows." Was she, then, to be always seeking, never finding?

She drew away from her brother and said bravely, "Where then shall I hide?"

"I can think of one place only," he said slowly. "Tomorrow, before daylight, I will take you there."

"And you, Ululani," said the princess, "must return to your own people, and never let yourself be seen by Makea."

Ululani shook her head. "I will go with you, *kamaliʻi wahine*. Your fortunes are mine."

In that predawn glow that is like memory of light, the princess's brother led the two girls along the beach. Round jutting rocks they went, where little waves slapped gently, and once through an archway formed by some forgotten lava flow. Here he turned in toward the land, and took them to a pool that was nearly concealed by a forest of *hau*.

"The tide is low," he said. "It will be a short swim only."

Taking his sister's hand, he led her into the water and to the far end of the pool. Only then could she see that, below the intertwining branches of *hau*, an undersea passage led inwards.

"We must swim underwater," he said, "but only for the distance of a deep breath. Come."

When the three raised their heads above the surface, reflected light of the newly-risen sun showed them a lofty cavern, round whose sides ran a shelf of rock.

Pulling herself up onto this, Popo'alaea said wonderingly, "Who would ever suspect that such a place existed? Makea will never find me here."

"This is Wai-'anapanapa," her brother said. "Few know of this secret cave."

For days the girls lived here. Ululani found stones to form a seat for the princess, and during the hot afternoons she stood behind her, fanning her with the *kahili*. At dusk each day, she swam out to receive the food brought to them by Popo'alaea's brother. On some evenings, the princess herself swam with silent strokes to the edge of the outer pool, and ran up and down the beach beyond. Always she had been accustomed to exercise, in her daily climbs of Pali-ku, and she could not bear to be idle.

Meanwhile, Makea had returned to find Popo'alaea and her attendant gone, and he went into a frenzy. He was like a man demented.

A story came to his ears that at a place beyond Hana, people were fearful because, at dusk, wraithlike figures were seen on the beach and among the trees.

"There are strange *akua* there," he was told. "The people are afraid to be abroad after sunset."

"*Akua!*" he repeated angrily. "Those are no ghosts! It is near where her brother lives."

He shouted for his adze, his prized one that was lashed to a stout handle, and ordered it to be sharpened to the finest of edges. Then, with his best warriors, he journeyed in the direction of Hana, full of rage.

On the way, they passed near the home of a *kaula*. Makea said: "We will stop here, and see what he says."

The *kaula* stood listening to the winds, and at length he said: "Go you to the top of Ka-'uiki Hill at dead of night. When a rainbow pierces the darkness it will be your guide, for it will be a royal rainbow."

Makea did as the prophet advised, and when the rainbow appeared in blackness of night, it was above a place not far from Popo'alaea's brother's home.

"I knew that was where she would go!" cried Makea.

He and his men hastened on their way and stormed through the area. Makea was insane with fury and jealousy. The brother was not to be found, and the chief felt sure that he must be with Popo'alaea. Actually, the brother was trying to find someone who could take his sister and Ululani by canoe to another island.

Makea and his warriors searched frantically for days, not knowing how near was their quarry, nor that several times Ululani ventured forth by night for food. Once the princess, too, came out of hiding to run on the beach, looking in the near-darkness like some being from the spirit world.

Late one afternoon Makea sat on the beach, exhausted, near a pool overhung with *hau* branches. The sun was sinking beyond Mauna Kahalawai, far across the water, and fiery arrows rayed upwards across the western sky.

The chief was not aware of this splendor, only of his raging, frustrating sense of loss. How terrible a thing it was to love a woman in this way! She had flaunted his manhood by running away from him, and had reduced him to a murderous, maniacal state.

He knew she was near, because he had seen the royal rainbow. But where? He had sought her everywhere. He turned from the blaze of sunset and stared into the pool. The water was so clear that he could see his face plainly. How frightened Popo'alaea would be, if confronted by such a face! His hands tightened on the handle of his adze, while he noticed, without realizing what he saw, that at the far side of the pool a cavern beyond reflected the colors of the late sun. A deep, quiet pool, a tranquil cavern—so still, so still.

With part of his mind he realized that something moved in the stillness. Frowning, absorbed by his anger, he was slow to understand what it was. Mirrored in the pool, in the cave beyond, a *kahili* waved rhythmically—a *kahili* that he recognized.

With a furious oath he sprang up, dived into the water and swam by the undersea passage into the inner pool. Popo'alaea sat on the shelf of rock, while the *kahili* in Ululani's hand swayed to and fro above her head, to cool her.

With a cry, the princess leapt back in terror. But there

was no escape. Makea reached her in an instant and struck her again and again with his adze, then turned on Ululani. Their blood flowed over the rocks, staining them forever, and dripped into the clear water—soon clear no longer, but streaked with red.

The bodies of the two girls sank to the bottom of the pool, and Makea glared down at them like a madman. The water had been ruffled by his headlong plunge, and a current stirred their long black hair, so that for a wild moment he thought they were still alive.

Even now, in certain lights, one can see in that pool the 'anapa, the brightness of prismatic colors that are sacred to divine chiefs. And on the night of Ku, god of justice, the glistening waters turn red as blood.

10

KA'ILI AND
THE OWL

Ka'ili and his sister, Na'ilima, lived with their parents in a valley near the tip of that section of Mauna Kahalawai that lies like an arm flung out upon the water.

The children loved to play in the sea that on calm days lapped the beach with a gentle touch, and during storms thundered against nearby cliffs to fall in showers of spray on the land above. On nights when the sea god was angry, Na'ilima would lie close to her brother, and together they would listen to his roars.

"Don't be afraid," Ka'ili would say. "We are safe in our snug grass house. And tomorrow, when the sea god is on his way home, he will have left behind good waves and we can surf."

One morning, when a storm was over but the surf still ran high, the two were resting on the beach after their favorite sport of riding the waves. As they sat there, Na'ilima was stringing a *lei* of the *'ilima* blossoms for which she had been named. Before the storm, she had gone up the slope of the mountain to gather the fragile golden flowers. They were, today, beginning to wilt. 'Ilima was so delicate!

All at once, an astonishing thing happened. A fleet of canoes came into sight around a rocky headland! So swiftly did it approach on the billowing sea that the children were still gazing in wonder when some men leapt ashore. They held long spears of *kauila* wood—they must be warriors!

Frightened now, the children started to run for home. But the men surrounded them, grabbed up the boy, and whisked him into one of the canoes.

Na'ilima ran screaming into the water after her brother, but in only a few moments the canoes were receding into the distance and she was left staring after them. When they had rounded the point, it might have been all a bad dream—except that Ka'ili was gone. Water swirled about her; the *'ilima* blossoms lay bright on the sand, forgotten.

Recovering from the shock of seeing her brother disappear, Na'ilima began to run along the shore after the canoes. Her father had gone down the beach looking for *'opihi*, little shellfish that cling to rocks. Her mother was in her *tapa* house, beating bark into *tapa* cloth. Both of them too far away to call—there just wasn't time! Following the path used by the king's messengers, Na'ilima ran around the end of the mountain and down the long stretch beyond, toward La-haina.

For most of the day she ran, always keeping the fleet in sight. She could see Ka'ili looking small and alone in the midst of the big men. Warriors! They must be the king's warriors. Who else?

At last they reached the harbor near where the king lived. Helplessly, she watched as her brother was taken to the dread *heiau* of Halulukoakoa, Roaring Thunder—the temple where human sacrifices were offered to the gods.

The people of that ancient time believed that this was what the gods wished. Some unlucky person had to be killed and placed on a temple altar. "I should have known!" thought Na'ilima in despair. "Why else would Ka'ili have been seized by the king's warriors?"

Poor Na'ilima went to a little distance from the town and sat on a broad, flat rock, and wept. What could a girl like herself do to rescue Ka'ili? Oh, why had her father been away? Why hadn't she taken the time to call her mother? She knew no one in this far-away town where the king lived. If only there were someone to whom she could turn! She tried to think what she should do, what her parents would tell her to do. Pray . . . pray to the family gods.

She sat praying for a long time, and at length became aware that a large owl had perched on the branch of a *kiawe* tree nearby. It was strange; she had just been supplicating Pueo, the owl god who was her family guardian.

The owl sat regarding her with round eyes that blinked solemnly, and she gazed back in fascination. Something about him did not seem like an ordinary owl.

After a time, he flapped to a branch closer to her. "Why are you crying, little girl?" he asked. "What is the matter?"

She realized then what it was that had seemed unusual about him. This was an owl who could see in daylight. And he could talk! Could it be . . .?

"My brother, Ka'ili, has been taken by the king's warriors to the terrible *heiau*," she said. "I will never see him again. On, poor, poor Ka'ili. Why did they have to take him?" She began to weep again.

"Now, now. Maybe there's something we can do." The owl flew still closer and lighted on a tree stump near her. "*Hu, hu,*" he said softly to himself, as if he were thinking deeply. Then he hooted, "I've got it! You sit right here on your big rock and keep on praying to the gods of your family. No god who has an interest in you will want anything to happen to Ka'ili, you know." He blinked at her —or had it been a wink?—and with a whirring of wings, flew off in the direction of the temple.

The gods of her family . . . one of them an owl. Na'ilima sat on her rock, praying, for what seemed an eternity. At last, she heard the sound of someone approaching. Looking up, she saw that a boy was coming toward her—but in the most peculiar manner. He was walking backwards! With the next breath, she saw that it was Ka'ili.

Joyfully, the brother and sister greeted each other, and he told her that the owl had made himself invisible and had flown into the temple.

"Oh, Ka'ili," Na'ilima said in awe. "I'm sure, I *know* it must be Pueo."

She glanced round to where the owl sat on his branch again. He let out a little hoot, as if he were laughing at her. "Don't stay talking here too long," he scolded.

But Ka'ili was intent on his story. "When he became visible again, to me anyway, he cut the ropes of *olona* fiber that were binding me, with his beak. After that, he started flying backwards. I didn't know what on earth he was doing! He didn't dare speak, because of the guards just outside. At last I realized that he wanted me to copy him, and walk backwards."

Ka'ili drew a long breath. "And that's how I came, all the way. The owl fluttered around at the other side of the temple, to distract the guards, while I got away."

With a sudden beating of wings, the owl flew over to them. "Quickly, now! You've been talking here too long! Under the rock, Ka'ili. And you, Na'ilima, sit on it again as if nothing were the matter."

Ka'ili was in a hollow under the rock in a flash, and Na'ilima sat on it, trying to look as if she were just sunning herself there.

In a moment, the temple guards rushed up to her. "Have you seen a boy anywhere?" they asked urgently. "Did he come this way?"

"A boy?" Na'ilima tried to still the trembling of her voice. "A boy? Let me see. I saw an owl a little while ago, but he flew away."

She was afraid then that she had said too much, but the men paid no attention to her remark about the owl. One of them had discovered Ka'ili's footprints in the sandy soil. With a shout, the guards were off, following the trail that led straight back to Halulukoakoa!

Na'ilima cried, "Oh, Pueo, how can we ever thank you? You *are* Pueo, aren't you?"

The owl said fussily, "Never mind thanks, or who I am. Along with you!"

But Na'ilima could see that he was smiling and that there was something like affection in those round, staring eyes. "Goodby, Pueo!" she cried. "We'll always remember you!" And she scampered after her brother.

Before the guards could return, angry at having been fooled, the children were well on the way to a safe hiding place in a far valley of Mauna Kahalawai.

HAWAIIAN ALPHABET AND PRONUNCIATION

There are twelve letters in the Hawaiian alphabet: the consonants *h, k, l, m, n, p, w,* and the five vowels.

The first six consonants are pronounced approximately as they are in English. The *w* is pronounced either as *w* or as *v*. The *v* sound comes more often after an *i* or an *e*, and sometimes at the beginning of a word.

Vowels are pronounced:

> *a* either as *a* in *above,* or as in *father*
> *e* either as *e* in *bet,* or as *a* in *late*
> *i* as *y* in *city*
> *o* as *o* in *sole*
> *u* as *oo* in *moon*

In such diphthongs as *ei, eu, oi, ou, ai, ae, ao,* and *au,* the stress is on the first letter, but the two letters are not so closely joined as they are in English.

The glottal stop (') in many of the words is peculiar to the Hawaiian language. It takes the place of a consonant, and indicates a break in the word, pronounced as in the English *oh-oh.* If the glottal stop comes at the beginning of a word, it indicates no slur or connection from the previous word.

GLOSSARY

'ahu'ula: feather cloak or cape, formerly worn by high chiefs and kings.

akua: god, goddess, spirit, ghost; divine, supernatural, godly. *Akua lapu*: evil spirit.

ali'i: chief, chiefess, king, queen, noble; royal, kingly.

'anapa: to shine, gleam, glitter, sparkle; brightness, gleam.

'ape'ape: huge-leafed forest perennial herbs, with thick stems rising to about four feet.

'awa: a shrub four to twelve feet tall with heart-shaped leaves, the root being the source of a narcotic drink of the same name.

e: O

'ele'io: to go speedily. The name of a famous runner on Maui.

ha: stalk that supports the leaf and enfolds the stem of certain plants, as *taro*.

hala: pandanus tree.

halau: longhouse, as for canoes.

hau: a lowland tree, with twisting branches and many roundshaped leaves.

heiau: pre-Christian place of worship.

hi'u: hind part or tail section of a fish.

hokeo: long gourd calabash, as used to contain fishing gear.

'ie'ie: an endemic woody, branching climber growing in forests at altitudes of about 1,500 feet.

'ilima: shrubs bearing yellow or orange flowers used in stringing *lei*.
imu: underground oven.

kahili: feathered standard, symbolic of royalty.
kahu: honored attendant, guardian, keeper.
kahuna: priest, minister, sorcerer.
kahuna nui: high priest.
kamali'i wahine: princess. *E ke kamali'i wahine*: O princess.
kapu: taboo, forbidden, sacred, consecrated.
kauila: a native tree. Its hard wood used for spears, tools.
kiawe: the algaroba tree, which grows in lowland areas.
koa: a tree of the acacia family. Its wood used for canoes, surfboards, calabashes.
koa'e-kea: white-tailed tropic bird, which inhabits cliffs of the high islands.
kukini: runner, swift messenger, as employed by chiefs of old.
kukui: candlenut tree.
ku'ula: any stone god used to attract fish, named for the god of fishermen; open altar near the sea for worship of fish gods.

lanai: porch, veranda. Temporary roofed construction with open sides.
lau: leaf, frond. To be much, many; very many, numerous; four hundred.
lau hala: pandanus leaf, especially as used in plaiting to make mats, baskets.
lei: garland, wreath.
limu: a general name for all kinds of plants living under water, both salt and fresh. *Limu-make*: deadly poisonous seaweed or moss.
lu'au: Hawaiian feast.

maile: a native twining shrub with shiny, fragrant leaves, used for decoration and *lei*.
malo: a man's or boy's loincloth.
mamane: a native leguminous tree, which thrives at high altitudes.
menehune: legendary race of small people who worked at night.

'ohelo: a small native shrub in the cranberry family.
'ohi'a-lehua: a tree with hard wood that grows at high altitudes (*'ohi'a*) and has red flowers (*lehua*).
olona: a native shrub whose bark was used for fiber in nets and cord. Cord of *olona* fiber.
'o'opu: one of the smallest of fish, which reaches the length of one inch.
'opae: shrimp.

'opihi: limpet, any of several species.

pali: cliff, precipice, steep hill.

pau: finished, ended, completed, over, all done.

pohaku 'ala: dense, waterworn volcanic stone.

poi: the Hawaiian staff of life, made usually from *taro* root, baked in an underground oven, and pounded with water.

po'i 'uhane: soul snatching. To capture the souls of living or dead persons, as by sorcery.

po'o: head.

puhi: eel.

pu'o'a: tower, steeple; house for depositing a corpse.

tapa or *kapa*: a cloth made from the inner bark of trees such as mulberry, and used for clothes or bedclothes.

taro or kalo: a plant with very large leaves, whose roots grow under water.

ulua: an important food fish.

wikiwiki: to hurry, hasten; quick.

Tuttle Books on Hawaii and the Pacific

JUVENILES:

Let's Learn Hawaiian *by Sibyl Hancock and Doris Sadler*

What's My Name in Hawaii? *by Louise Bonner; illustrated by Ray Lanterman*

The Secret Cave of Kamanawa *by Helen Berkey; illustrations by Ray Lanterman*

The Voyage of the Flying Bird *by Margaret Titcomb*

Aunty Pinau's Banyan Tree *by Helen Berkey; illustrations by Ray Lanterman*

COOKERY:

Hawaiian Cuisine *by members of the Hawaii State Society of Washington, D.C.*

Hawaii Cooks *by Maili Yardley*

FICTION:

Haiku of Hawaii *by Annette Schaefer Morrow*

Hawaii: End of the Rainbow *by Kazuo Miyamoto*

HISTORY:

The Hawaiians: An Island People *by Helen Gay Pratt; drawings by Rosamond S. Morgan and Juliette May Fraser*

Hawaii's Story by Hawaii's Queen *by Liliuokalani*

Calabashes and Kings: An Introduction to Hawaii *by Stanley D. Porteus*

Ancient Hawaiian Civilization: A Series of Lectures Delivered at the Kamehameha Schools (revised) *by E. S. Craighill Handy and Others*

Lawrence M. Judd and Hawaii: An Autobiography *by Lawrence M. Judd, as told to Hugh W. Lytle*

The Hawaiian Chief's Children's School 1839–1850 *by Mary A. Richards*

Islands of Destiny *by Olive Wyndette*
Surfing: The Sport of Hawaiian Kings *by Ben R. Finney and James D. Houston*
Incidents of a Whaling Voyage *by Francis Allyn Olmsted*
An Account of the Polynesian Race: Its Origin and Migrations *by Abraham Fornander*
Missionary Adventures in the South Pacific *by David and Leona Crawford*
Guam Past and Present *by Charles Beardsley*
A Complete History of Guam *by Paul Carano and Pedro C. Sanchez*
The Drama of Fiji: A Contemporary History *by Dr. John Wesley Coulter*

LANGUAGE:

Dictionary of the Hawaiian Language *by Lorrin Andrews*
An English-Hawaiian Dictionary: With Various Useful Tables *by H. R. Hitchcock*
Hawaiian Phrase Book
A Short Synopsis of the Most Essential Points in Hawaiian Grammar *by W. D. Alexander*

MANNERS AND CUSTOMS:

Myths and Legends of the Polynesians *by Johannes E. Andersen*
Polynesian Researches (4 Volumes) *by William Ellis*
Hawaii Goes Fishing *by Jean Scott MacKellar*
Hawaiian Legends of Old Honolulu
Hawaiian Legends of Ghosts and Ghost-Gods
Hawaiian Legends of Volcanoes
The Legends and Myths of Hawaii: The Fables and Folk-lore of a Strange People *by His Hawaiian Majesty Kalakaua*

MUSIC AND DANCE:

The Unwritten Literature of Hawaii: The Sacred Songs of the Hula *collected and translated by Nathaniel B. Emerson*
Folk Songs Hawaii Sings *compiled, arranged and annotated by John M. Kelly, Jr.; illustrated by Keichi Kimura*
Hawaii: Music in Its History *by Ruth Hausman*

NATURAL HISTORY:

Hawaiian Herbs of Medicinal Value *by D. M. Kaaiakamanu and J. K. Akina; trans. by Akaiko Akana*

Poisonous Plants of Hawaii *by Harry L. Arnold*

Manual of Wayside Plants of Hawaii *by Willis T. Pope*

Hawaiian Flowers and Flowering Trees *by Loraine E. Kuck and Richard C. Tongg*

Tropical Gardening: A Handbook for the Home Gardener *by Peggy Hickok Hodge*

Hawaiian Land Mammals *by Raymond J. Kramer*

Birds of Hawaii *by George C. Munro*

Precious Stones *by Dr. Max Bauer; translated by L. J. Spencer*

The Book of Opals *by Wilfred Charles Eyles*

Sea Shells of the World with Values *by A. Gordon Melvin*

Pacific Sea Shells *by Spencer Wilkie Tinker*

A Guide to Shell Collecting in the Kwajalein Atoll *by Fred B. Brost and Robert D. Coale*

TRAVEL AND PICTORIAL:

The Hawaiian Guide Book for Travelers *by Henry M. Whitney*

Going Native in Hawaii: A Poor Man's Guide to Paradise *by Timothy Head*

Bachelor's Hawaii *by Boye de Mente*

Polynesia in Colour *by James Siers*

The Boy Travellers in Australasia *by Thomas W. Knox*

MISCELLANEOUS:

Menehune Magic of How to Swim *by Leo Lynne*

Coconut Palm Frond Weaving *by William Goodloe*

Hawaii's Religions *by John F. Mulholland*

CHARLES E. TUTTLE COMPANY: PUBLISHERS

Rutland, Vermont & Tokyo, Japan